One Day in the Life of Edmund

By
WENDELL A. THOMAS

Publisher:
Wendell A. Thomas; 547 Judson Ave.; Evanston, IL 60202

ISBN:
Library of Congress Control Number: 2023920412

Recommended citation:
Thomas, Wendell A. 2023. Stories of Life. Publisher: Wendell A. Thomas, Evanston, Illinois.
Cover art by W. Thomas

To

My Dear Family

I'll begin this way.

The pencil makes a rubbing sound on the paper when she writes. This is how I started. Or should I say that is how I started. This, or that, I don't know. I look at her to see if she is annoyed. She doesn't look annoyed. Are you?

She looks at me but doesn't say anything.

I continue. I suppose that if you were to make a judgment, or even to have an opinion about something that you didn't know anything about up until now, you would have to have some information about all the crap that went on before. I think that makes sense, yes?

Will you write down every word that you say, too?

She looks at me and nods.

Her name is Tammy Rothchild and she sits across the desk from me, writing.

You're writing everything?

She nods again.

I give her a look but she smiles.

Tammy's a pretty big lady and we're sitting in her office. She's looking at me and I'm looking back. It's not a romantic thing for either of us. At least not for me anyway.

Maybe it is for her even though she's about twice my age and even though I really don't find her very appealing.

She's wearing a tan cashmere sweater that tends to show-off her breasts, which are large. Around her neck is a double strand of strung pearls. She has a gold earring dangling from each ear and a barrette in her hair which is dark and wavy. The barrette keeps her hair from falling across her forehead.

Her age could be a very sexy thing. I'm seventeen and she's probably somewhere in her thirties. That type of relationship could be very, very sexy to get involved in if the other person happens to be more appealing than Miss Rothchild.

"Look, Edmond," she says, "if you don't talk straight with me then I don't think this will do any good."

She gives me her smile.

I trust her, kind of. She has a broad face and a full smile. I mean her smile is big and genuine. It lights up her whole face when she uses it, which is often.

She keeps writing.

Did you write down that stuff about your weight and your breasts?

"Yes, Edmund. I'm writing everything you say."

I wanted to be sure that I understood her.

You want me to just talk and talk and talk. My whole life story, right? Or anything I feel like saying, right?

"That's right," she said. Okay.

I'm thinking.

I'll start in the bathroom, that's the first thing I remember.

The bathroom had small tiles, each one no larger than a quarter. The ones behind the sink and the toilet were whiter than the rest. Each tile was bordered by a dark line of pencil-thin grout. The tiles that were underfoot were grey and they always felt gritty under the soles of my shoes. But when I crawled on the floor, sliding my palms around, they felt smooth. It was strange. And whenever I bent to pick something up from the floor, they felt smooth. It always seemed magical.

Is this what you mean?

"Continue," she said, "you're doing just fine."

The porcelain sink sat on a column that tapered down to a larger base. The column was a bright, shiny white, much different from the sink itself which always had water dripping from the hot water spigot. The water ran a path to the drain, making a yellow-brown stain that never came out even though it was regularly scrubbed with a rag, hot water and a course cleanser.

Above the sink was the medicine cabinet with the mirror and the light with a string attached. To the left was the tub with the worn porcelain that I wished were smooth and slick so that I could slide around better when I took my bath.

When I was in the tub, my mother took Ivory soap and lathered it in her hands and then dunked her hands, leaving the soap bubbles floating. They were destroyers and aircraft carriers and PT boats. I could bring my hand down like a big bomb and smack the ships, sinking them and getting soap in my eyes at the same time. My mother would wipe my eyes with the wet washcloth and I would maneuver my hands under the water, with just my fingertips showing. I would pretend they were the sailors from the sunken ships. I would maneuver them around until I could get them safely onto some of the floating debris. I was always able to save these finger-tip sailors moments before the sharks and whales came to eat them.

There was a radiator too. It hissed and whistled during the cold months. It hissed and it banged. I thought there was a hammer inside of the pipes that banged away at them to make the noise.

On this day I was in the bathroom for a different reason. The radiator was off. It was spring. It must have been early May.

I was standing on the toilet seat aiming a pistol at the ceiling and then pulling the trigger. *WHAM!* The dart hit the ceiling and stuck. My grandmother handed me another dart. *WHAM!* She had pure white hair. Her name was, "Gram." It was later, I don't know how much, that I came to understand that Gram was my own mother's mother.

"This is rubber," she said. She was holding a dart, fingering the rim of the suction cup. Rubber. That is my first memory.

That is when my life began.

Of course, other things had happened in my life before that.

To have heard my father tell it, as a baby, I never slept. I only ate and screamed for more. No way to shut me up. Loudest damn kid.

On this day, though, I was a good boy. Me and Gram. Home alone in the bathroom. As the darts would lose their suction and fall, Gram would pick them up and hand them to me. *WHAM! WHAM! WHAM! WHAM!* It was louder and more fun to do this in the bathroom. **WHAM! WHAM!** Besides I couldn't be so big if I didn't have the toilet seat to stand on.

And then the buzzing started.

Gram said, "They're home now! Come, Edmund," and she left the bathroom and pushed the button in the hallway that opened the door below.

It was my mother, Lillian, and my father, Edmund. They were both smiling and laughing and carrying things.

My mother was carrying an armful of blankets. Inside the blankets was my new baby brother, Robert.

My mother leaned over and showed me his face. I didn't know what to make of him.

A tiny little face with closed eyes and funny looking pink skin. I put my hand on top of my head, feeling my hair. He didn't have any.

"Give him a kiss, Edmund," she said.

I didn't want to kiss him.

"Give him a kiss," my father said.

Until then, everything had been so nice. I didn't want them to be home. I wanted to be in the bathroom playing with my dart gun, and Gram handing me the darts. *WHAM! WHAM! WHAM!*

"Kiss your brother!" my father said.

I didn't. Instead, I raced to the bathroom and got my dart gun and darts and hurried into the bedroom, putting them on the floor under my dresser where they would be safe.

★★★★★★★★★★★★★★

Gram was nice. Perfume, rosy cheeks, white hair and bracelets. She must have had a dozen silver and gold bracelets that slid up and down her arm.

Gram was rich, too. I found that out when I was about five, old enough to cross streets by myself. Whenever she came to visit, she would give me a dollar and send me off to the drugstore. I didn't have to do anything to earn it either, just sort of hang around and wait. Maybe watch her smoke a few of her long thin cigarettes, but I didn't mind that. She would blow big puffs of smoke into the room. There was so much smoke that floated into the room from just one puff. She could do smoke rings too. She could blow a smoke ring toward me and I could try to stick my hand through the hole to have a bracelet that would drift up my arm and lose shape before it got to my shoulder.

She was big compared to me but not nearly as large as the other big people in my life. She talked loudly, and often, and then leaned forward and laughed at what she had said.

She laughed loudly and tried to talk while she laughed which seemed to make her laugh even more. She was fun.

My father used to tell my mother that Gram was crazy.

Sometimes, on a Sunday we would take a drive to visit Gram and my mother's sister, Aunt Gertrude, who was married to Uncle Harry. They were both nice. Everybody at Gram's was nice except for my fat cousin, Lorraine, who was two years older than me, and she was a brat.

Lorraine never wanted to eat at the children's table out in the kitchen. She always wanted to be around the adults.

One Sunday when we were visiting, eating an afternoon dinner, she tore off a piece of her heavily buttered roll and threw it at me. It hit me on the chest and clung until the butter couldn't hold it anymore and then it rolled down my shirt and onto my lap. She thought that was really funny. She giggled and laughed and tossed her head from side to side.

I grabbed a handful of peas and let them fly. They hit her face, her dress and stuck to her hair. I laughed my loud laugh, the one I used when I only making noise. I threw my head back and forth and looked at the ceiling where the cord with the switch dangled from the fixture above. The ceiling was a clean, bright white. There was a shadow, a circular shadow, just above the fixture, surrounding the metal cap that held the light globe.

Lorraine began crying and made an angry face. She got up from her chair and came around the table to my side. I kept on laughing and fat Lorraine let me have it right in the face. She really smacked me a good one. There was an instant of red in my vision and I found myself looking at the wall next to the table.

Then I was after her. I wasn't strong enough to make her go down but she did stumble backward, hitting her arm on the door frame that led to the dining room. She was quiet for a couple of seconds and then she let out a long howl.

"You come here!" It was my father, standing in the doorway, filling the space.

He was a big, thick muscled man with a huge stomach and two chins. He was very tall with big hands and he could pick me up and do anything he wanted with me.

My mother had told me that I was her big-boy. But compared to him I was nothing.

He could out-run me and out-think me and out-fox me. He could do everything better than I could. And he could spank me very hard when he felt like it, which seemed often.

He could take the hairbrush with the wooden back and the long handle and he could really give it to me. He could march me into our bathroom and tell me to bend over. My pants would be down and I would be bent over the bathtub, waiting, the drain to the right and the soap holder in front of my head, across the tub. And there would be this feeling in my stomach. Nausea

His hitting me was always a shock. Of course, I knew it was coming, but still, it was always a shock. Does that make sense? It jarred my ass. My hips would be against the cold porcelain and when he would hit me the cold would go through my skin and right to the bone.

The smack that I heard didn't seem connected to me. And then a few seconds later it did. First it burned and then it stung. Then it hurt. But what made me want to throw-up was knowing I was going to get it and there was no way out. If I tried to run, he could catch me. If I struggled against him, I would be jerked around and thrown to the floor.

I screamed in my mind.

Enough! Don't do it again. I'll be good. I'll be very good! Please don't do it again.

Mom! Mom! Can't you hear?

I was always afraid that if I screamed out loud, he would hit me harder, to quiet me. I could picture my mother sitting in the living room, always right on the edge of her chair, poised and ready at any moment to come in and hit the bastard. She would probably hit him with the big iron skillet that she would run to the kitchen and get. I could see the look on her face, realizing that something was happening to her big-boy and, momentarily, she would throw down her book or dump whatever it was that she had in her hands and come running. She would smash my father senseless and make him bleed and he could die. Then, when it was peaceful, she and I could go to the neighborhood sweet store for a treat.

But she never did.

My father led me into Gram's bedroom. I didn't want to get it in there. It seemed like a worse place with all the relatives sitting in the dining room. They would hear me getting it. *Whack! Whack! Whack!* And fat Lorraine would hear too.

He pointed to the white wooden chair sitting in the bedroom. "You sit there,[11] he said.

It was okay. I was glad we were at Gram's.

The chair wasn't so bad for a while. But then it became more difficult as I heard the plates being cleared and the coffee being served along with the pie and ice cream. All the while, my fat cousin asking if she couldn't help with this or that.

Would anyone like to see the drawing she had made during art period at school? I think she was in first grade.

I wanted to go to the other side of the room and look in the dresser drawers.

The family moved further away, into the front room that had the large oriental rug and the piano and the alcove that overlooked the street. Everybody in the other room was having fun and eating desert.

Uncle Harry told a joke and everybody laughed.

I slipped down from the chair and started quietly across the slick linoleum floor, sliding my feet. I pulled open the top drawer. There was a small black box and I took it out and put it on the bed. Inside the box were some rings with little sparkling stones and some earrings with big sparkling stones. Some of them were the same colors as some of the clear marbles I had at home. None of the rings fit. They were too big for my fingers and too big for my thumbs.

I took each large stone and examined it, holding it close to my face and looking at the reflection of the room in the stone. I took two stones and put them each close to an eye and looked toward the window. I rubbed them on the bedspread to polish them and then licked them and rubbed them some more.

When I looked up, my father was standing in the door. He was huge the way he filled the space. I closed the box and quickly put it on top of the dresser and got back on the chair.

"Put it back where you found it," he said.

I looked at the dresser and saw that the drawer was still open. "I'll deal with you later," he said, and turned and walked away. A voice floated through the house and through the walls.

It was my mother's voice. "Oh my, Lorraine, that's a lovely drawing. Ohh, mm.

Yes, that's simply lovely, dear."

It was dark when we left for home. My brother was in the front seat sleeping across my mother's lap. My parents talked quietly, sometimes using the alphabet to spell out words they didn't want me to know they were using.

My father looked over at my mother and she turned her head from the road and looked at him. From the back seat I could see their faces turned towards each other. They both had hats on. My mother's hat was dark, a purple color with a feather or two that went from the front to the back and stuck out behind the side of her head.

"Yes, sir," my father said. "Robert is a good boy. He's already smarter than," and then he nodded his head toward me, "and he's not even a year." He laughed and looked back to the road and then the talked some more, spelling words from time to time.

I wiggled my legs a little. Back and forth quietly knocking my knees together. After a few minutes I gave up and peed in my pants. I didn't care.

My father. If I hadn't been so afraid of him, I could have hated him. But I was afraid.

I was so afraid of him that I loved him.

When I first peed in my pants it felt warm and cozy, kind of. It felt okay. Now, though, it was making my thighs feel itchy and my underwear was getting cold.

I watched the moon.

It kept even with us the whole way home, traveling at our speed, ducking in and out from the clouds and stopping when there was a red light. I looked away and counted to ten and then looked back. There it was, staying with us. I thought that maybe the moon was playing this game just for me.

My parents kept talking and spelling. They could have their secrets. I didn't care. I had one of my own. I sat watching, looking away and then looking back again and again, never saying anything, keeping quiet about me and the moon.

I thought I must be special, that the moon would follow me home exactly like it did. It made me feel really important that something as far off and as big as the moon would be concerned so about me. I wondered if the moon was trying to send me a message, trying to tell me something. I thought that I could almost hear a voice, a quiet, deep commanding voice. I wondered if the moon was trying to tell me that I was special. More special, maybe, than any other boy in the world and that I was very wonderful and that soon everyone was going to discover how wonderful I was.

★★★★★★★★★★★★★★★

I used to have this picture running through my head.

I could see myself walking along the street. I wasn't in my own neighborhood where almost everybody lived in apartments. I was on a street where there was sunlight and houses. There were no apartments. There were small trees out in front of the houses and along the parkways on either side of the street. In the front yards there were tricycles and large rubber balls. Inflated balls, under pressure so that when you kicked them, they flew far and bounced high. As I walked along the street people opened their front doors, and their storm doors too, and they yelled.

"Hello, Edmund! How are you today?"

I would look at them wave and yell back, "Fine! I'm fine!"

★★★★★★★★★★★★★★★★

"Is Mommy's big-boy going to be a good helper for daddy?" my mother said. I was all dressed up and going down to my father's office on a work day.

We had a shiny black Mercury with soft, grey cushioned seats that grabbed my corduroy pants. It was a car that my father loved. I got in the front seat with my father. In the front, between the two of us was a rod with a black knob on the end. It was the gear shift and it came up from the floor between our seats. My father would drive a little way and then he would take hold of the knob and move the rod in one direction or another.

"What is that?" I said. "It's a gearshift," he said.

"What does it do?" I said.

"It makes the car go faster," he said. "Here, put your hand on it and I'll show you."

I put my hand on it and he put his hand on top of mine. As we went along, every so often he would push the pedals on the floor and move the rod in that knowing way that he had.

I could see buildings and trees and people and traffic lights. There were traffic lights as far as I could see and they were all green at the same time. Then they were all red. I had never known that about traffic lights.

I said, "Who makes them change all together?" He laughed.

Then, all of a sudden, the lake was on one side of us for as far as I could see. There were big puffy clouds in the sky that looked like giant pillows all fluffed up and the very blue sky everywhere that the clouds were not. There were boats too. Boats with big white sails out on the lake.

And cars. There were cars in front of us and behind us and on the sides of us. We were all whizzing along going to work.

In his office, high above the ground, there were some big green metal cabinets and two desks. A typewriter was set on the top of one of the desks and there was a woman sitting at that desk.

"Evelyn," my father said, "this is Edmund. Evelyn is my secretary, Edmund."

"Junior," she said, and then she smiled.

She had bright red lips and large red earrings.

She gave me some paper and a pencil and made a place for me on top of a wood chair. She put some magazines on my lap and I started drawing. I drew for a very long time. I drew pictures of the lake and the boats and pictures of the cars zooming along the road to take home to give to my mother. And I made pictures of traffic lights and tall buildings and flags.

Evelyn got up from her desk and went over and stood behind him. She whispered something in his ear and they laughed.

I had to go to the bathroom.

"You're just like your father, Junior," she said, and then she laughed again.

Evelyn took me down the hall, her high heels clicking on the marble floor. She went into the room with me. There was a large door that I could have crawled under because it did not reach down to the floor.

"You go right in there," she said, pointing at the door. She laughed. "Do you want me to hold your little pee-pee for you?"

I sat on the toilet and all I could see were her legs, waiting outside the door. I pushed quietly, holding my breath and then I took a wad of paper from the roll, very slowly, so that she wouldn't hear.

I looked down at myself.

It didn't look so little to me. Of course, compared to my father's, it was very little. I had showered with my father and I knew what he looked like. Who would want one like his, surrounded by all of that fuzzy, curly hair? His was scary looking.

When we got back to the office my father said it was time for lunch.

Downtown was fun, except for Evelyn. My father's office was fun. He, busy on the phone and me drawing all of the pictures for my mother. There was the car ride and the boats, and now I was going to ride an elevator by myself. And I was going to eat in a restaurant all by myself. It was fun to be at work.

There were other people sitting along the counter and they were eating too. I held the edge of the counter and gave myself a good pull and spun around on the stool while everything in the room zipped past my eyes. Once, twice, three times I went around. I ate another bite of my sandwich and then spun again. And again.

All of a sudden there was this crashing, shattering noise. My plate had flown off the counter and smashed onto the floor, the sandwich and potato chips were scattered and strewn across the aisle.

Everyone was looking at me.

Then this man in a dark suit was standing next to me.

"They have no sense to leave a kid like you alone," the man said. "Who's gonna pay for this?"

I didn't know. My father had given Evelyn the money. Didn't she pay? She was supposed to pay.

I slid off the stool and started making my way to the door, between the counter and the tables, hoping the man wasn't going to grab me from behind. Everyone pretended not to watch.

The corridor on the eighteenth floor was long and dark with lights hanging down from the ceiling, their yellow globes glowing. The office doors lined the long hallway. I walked slowly, trying to remember which one was my father's. They all looked the same. I stopped at one door and listened, but I couldn't hear my father's voice. Then I saw the mail slot. I lifted it quietly and looked inside.

I moved along the hall, carefully lifting each brass flap on each of the mail slots. I wanted to hurry because the man in the dark suit might be coming. If I could get into the office before he found me out in the hallway it would feel safer. Evelyn could tell him that she paid. My father could tell him that he gave Evelyn the money. He would believe them, I was sure.

And then, ahh, I recognized the desks. My father's suit coat was draped over the chair at Evelyn's desk. I tried the knob. The door was locked. I lifted the flap on the mail slot again and looked around. I couldn't see them, but I could hear something. They were making noise somewhere in the office. I stood on my tiptoes and then I could see them.

They were over in the corner, on the floor. I thought they were wrestling and that he was winning because he was on top of her. Of course, I knew how strong he was.

Then my father stood up and I saw him pulling his pants up and buckling them.

Something was wrong.

Evelyn stood up and brushed at her dress. She took her shoes from the file cabinet and put them on. They stood close to each other and kissed and I went across the hall and sat against the wall.

I hated her.

I wanted to be home giving my drawings to my mother and watching her smile while she told me how beautiful they were.

I sat and waited. Later, the door clicked as my father came out of the office. "Edmund," he said, "how long have you been there?" He looked different. I didn't feel well.

When we left, I climbed into the back seat. I didn't want to move his gear shift around and I didn't want his hand on top of mine. I didn't want to see the boats or the other cars or anything else.

I knew that I didn't ever want to go to my father's office again.

★★★★★★★★★★★★★★★★

"Well," Tammy says. She puts the legal pad that she's holding on the chair next to her and lays the pencil down on top of it. "Edmund, I want to do this with you, but you will have to tell the truth. I don't need an exercise in writing, really."

I look at her.

I am.

"Well," she says, "what is all this about me sitting behind a desk being a therapist or psychiatrist? Is that what's happening here?"

I look around the room. I'm lying in a bed and she is sitting in a chair at the side of the bed. There is another bed in the room but it's not occupied although there have been different people in it from time to time. Older people. Everybody where I am is older. I'm the youngest one in the whole place. In fact, it is an old people's home. A nursing home. And it often smells like urine in the hall and in my room too.

I wet my bed sometimes when they don't get me to the bathroom often enough.

They've got these adult diapers that they use on me so they don't have to change the sheets so often. Sometimes I get rashes from staying wet too long.

Tammy keeps writing.

My eyes jerk about. I don't have too much control over them. They've been hurt, damaged, just like the rest of me.

"Are we here in the nursing home?" she says.

Yes, but what about the other people? How can you spend all this time with me? What about them?

"Barbara said it's okay. If there's a problem, they will come and get me," she said.

Barbara? You mean the one with the binoculars for glasses and the thick ankles?

"Well," she says, "I never noticed her ankles, but yes. The head of the nursing staff."

Huh, I didn't know she was the head of it all.

"Edmund, you understand, don't you? About being straight," she said. Yes.

But, Tammy, she doesn't understand everything. She doesn't understand that I really saw her sitting across the desk from me in an office. Her office. That's where I thought we were. Her, sitting there looking at me, smooth olive skin, arms resting easily on her desk, writing. And the sweater, accentuating her breasts. The V at the neck showing just the right amount of cleavage.

Did you write that about the cleavage?

"Yes," she says. "I told you I would write everything. [11]

Now, when I look at her, I can see that she is wearing her white nurse's outfit and she doesn't have a sweater on and there are no strung pearls around her neck and there is no barrette in her hair, but rather, a small white nurse's cap on her head. She still has the warm smile and the smooth skin.

"Are you seventeen?" she says.

No.

"How old are you, Edmund?" she says.

Twenty-seven. I don't want to fight with her. I want her to do this talking thing with me. Besides, if you want to know the truth, I don't have too much else to do with my life.

"Why are you here?" she says.

Even if God wants me here, that's not what Tammy wants to hear. She sits in the chair looking at me, waiting. She has me trapped. Don't you?

"No," she says, "I don't have you trapped."

Tammy can decipher the words that I say. The doctors and other nurses can't do it. I don't know why she can and they can't. Even if I wanted to, I couldn't tell them about the secret that Tammy and I share.

She smiles.

She says that she feels very special about it. Special about me. She calls it, "our special secret." And, would I mind if we keep it a secret? Not at all. Why would I? At least she asks.

Some other people around here, they don't really give a rat's ass how I'm feeling. Tammy frowns at me.

It's true god-damnit! You want me to talk straight and honest and then you frown when I don't say what you want me too. Right?

"Wrong," she says. "It's not that. It was a frown of pain. To think that you feel, or have the sense from the way you are treated here that you are not cared for. As far as my feelings about you are concerned, nothing could be further from the truth."

On days when I have trouble, some of them have talked about how they sure won't miss me when they're gone. Or when I am either.

Tammy's different. She cares about me. For all the time that she's been here and been my nurse on the night shift, she's been kind.

"Three years and four months,[11] she says.

We look at each other and smile a little.

She wonders sometimes if I would like to have a story read to me. Or would I like to play a game of twenty questions? Is there something that I would like to talk about?

Still, I can't see our relationship becoming any more than what it already is. I mean, of course, if I could get up and walk and if I could talk in normal way and if I had a job of some sort. Like if I was a school teacher. If I was something normal and if I met her in a bar or her car broke down on the highway and I stopped to help and we hit it off, then maybe something would happen with us. But not now. We're just going to be friends and leave it at that.

It's strange how Tammy has been able to understand me for months. "For more than a year, Edmund," she says.

Edith Hankins, one of the nurses, says, "Come on Edmund, say it slowly. Say it clearly. Try not to slur so much. Use your tongue."

You know Edith. Well, on one of her shifts, she brings this portable tape recorder and asks me some questions and I answer them while she holds the recorder close to my mouth. After she asks some questions, she pushes the buttons and plays it back. I hear her ask a question and then I hear another voice, it doesn't sound like me though. They were sounds of a sort, but really, they weren't words that I could understand.

Edith says, "See? Do you see, Edmund? Do you see why we can't make out what you say?" She chuckles.

Of course, in my mind I don't have any difficulty at all. I can hear every word clearly.

Only when I try to talk is there any problem.

My tongue gets in the way. I can feel my tongue just fine, sitting there where it always has, resting in my mouth. But I can't move it very well. The son-of-a-bitch just won't move the way it should to make the words.

I don't know how Tammy Rothchild does it, making out my words and all.

It was Edith, but it might have been anybody talking to me, including my brother,

Robert, who has only been here twice in the time that I have been lying in this God-damned bed or sitting in the God-damned wheelchair that they put me into every day. They strap me in and I sit in the hall along with all of the others. Some no longer make it to the hall for the day of sitting. They are in their beds full-time. The next step is the ambulance and they cover them up and haul them off to the funeral home. It happens pretty regularly. The people lining the halls become the older, the more invalided, and eventually, the crazies whose families have sent them here to die.

My mother, though, she didn't send me here to die. She comes to visit when she can, which is usually twice a week. We spend some time together and she talks about what she's doing with her church. She's on two or three different committees.

She's a saint, really. Never says anything unkind about anyone. She has a way of looking on the bright side of things and pulling out some good from everything.

Like, even me and this permanent situation that I'm in, she refers to as, "A temporary setback." It's wonderful. Wonderful for me to see her face light up and fill with hope.

And it's not easy for her to get here. It's a two-hour bus ride, with transfers and all, from the time she leaves the apartment until she gets here.

Does she complain? Never. She's walked in on days when it's storming, when nobody else has anyone to visit them. You should see the look on the nurses' faces when she walks in on a day like that.

"Edmund," Tammy says, "why are you here? Answer me, please." My eyes settle down and I am able to focus on her.

I had a stroke.

"What kind?" she says.

A heat stroke.

"How long have you been here?" she says.

Five years.

She smiles at me and begins to ready herself to leave.

A major, severe-fucking-brain-damaging-motor-function-ing heat stroke. As big a fucking heat stroke as you can have without actually dying. And a good amount of the time I wish I would have.

Tammy stops smiling and gives me a look that I'm not sure about.

"It means that there are times that I feel so bad for you that it tears at me," she says. "Sometimes I just admire you so much."

What's to admire?

"Oh, just you, I suppose," she says. "Just the fact that there are parts of you that don't work all of the time and that there are parts of you that don't seem to work any of the time but that you keep on trying. That I think you're warm and loving and appreciative. Does that answer your question?"

I don't know. You said too much. You're making me nervous.

"Well," she says, "you know I think you're handsome, also."

Hey, come on. Don't do that!

"Don't do what?" she says.

Don't talk that way to me.

"Why not?" she says.

Because.

"Because, why?" she says.

I don't know! Maybe because you're lying and I can't get away from you.

"Am I? Am I lying, Edmund?" she says.

★★★★★★★★★★★★★★★★

She goes into the bathroom to use the toilet and wash her face. The paper towels that she used to *dry* her hands went into the waste container in the bathroom with a heavy thud.

Are you mad at me?

"No," she says.

She doesn't look to be, but the noise the towels made in the bathroom made me wonder.

Did you use my toothpaste?

She laughs and shakes her head. "No, I didn't, Edmund, and I did not slam the towels into the waste container, either."

Well, why do you laugh then?

"Well, Edmund, you make me laugh. I laugh because I like you." She came over to the bed and leaned over and kissed my forehead.

Why did you do that?

"Guess," she said.

Don't do that.

"All right. I'm sorry. I like you," she said.

Not in that way, you don't.

"Edmund, I'll see you tonight. At eleven," she said.

★★★★★★★★★★★★★★★★

Time flies doesn't it, Tammy? Edith just left and here you are, back again. I'm glad to see you.

Tammy stares at me.

Please don't stare. I know I look pretty bad. Maybe like I've been beaten up. I'll get to it. They didn't hold a mirror up for me, so I haven't seen it.

And please don't say anything until I finish what I have to say. Don't say one fucking word if you please.

Just write.

★★★★★★★★★★★★★★★★

There is no clock in my room, but when you leave and the new shift comes on, I know that it is seven a.m.

Miriam Samuelson comes into my room a few minutes after you left and I am trying to feign sleep in the hope that she will look in on me and leave. I have been up for the better part of the night. It's too hard and it takes too long to roll from my back to my side, so I just close my eyes as I see the door to my room begin to open.

She walks across the room and turns the long plastic rod that connects to the top of the blinds, letting in the morning light but not the sun as the window is on the west side of the room. She picks up a piece of paper from the floor and crumples it in her hand. It makes a noise when it lands against the bottom of the empty metal trash can against the wall. She pauses at the foot of the bed, looking at me, I suppose, and then she moves the few steps to my bathroom and goes in. The large bathroom door doesn't make any noise when she opens it, but I can tell that she opens it because it causes the air in the room to change.

Even though no one is talking there is a change in the loudness of the room. I can hear the cloth of her uniform brush against itself when she steps into the bathroom and before the door closes. The sound of her clothing rubbing against itself is further away, and yet it sounds louder than if she were next to my bed doing something. I've noticed it before and find myself thinking that it is like the quiet roar of a conch seashell. It is that deafening roar of nothing.

I can hear Miriam urinating. Sometimes, before she uses my bathroom, I can hear the toilet paper being unrolled and tom off. When she does it that way she probably drops the paper into the bowl and pees on the paper. Those are the times when she is concerned that she might wake me from a sleep. Today she is not concerned. I wish that she were.

When she finishes, I hear the rustling of her clothing while she pulls up her panties and brushes down her dress. The flushing of the toilet is loud and powerful, sucking down the liquid from the bowl and filling it fresh. The spigot goes on and water runs into the sink briefly. The spigot has an aerator on its' nozzle. The noise that it makes is so much more than what it gives. When they have me in the bathroom and they're filling the sink, the noise that the water makes is so loud, with the water first hitting the porcelain and then roiling into itself in the basin that I am always surprised at how slowly it fills.

Then there are two pushes on the soap dispenser. When her hands are washed, the paper towels, all four of them, are pulled from the dispenser and she dries herself. The door to the bathroom is opened and I hear her step into the room.

She uses four paper towels to dry her hands. Why does she need four, I wonder, when she only has to dry her hands. When she washes my face and my hands, she only uses three.

She's unlike my mother, that's for sure.

When my mother visits me and she has to go to the bathroom, she uses two towels. Just two. She doesn't need four or six or ten God-damned towels to dry her hands. She only needs two.

That's the way her life is. She doesn't need more. In fact, she needs less. She doesn't ask for things. She doesn't need another coat or more gloves or new dresses. She makes-do with what she has. She's not into everybody to see what it is that she can get for herself.

I don't know if it makes sense the way I'm saying it. Let's say that my mother is on her way to go do something and let's say that I live at home with her. Suppose that the two of us were planning on going to a movie and she had one of her headaches. She gets these ferocious headaches from time to time. Maybe they're migraines, I'm not sure. Anyway, she probably wouldn't even say anything about having a head-ache. We would just go to the movie. Well, if you want to know the truth, we might have to leave the movie a little early if her headache got too severe or something like that. But even if we stayed for the whole movie and then when we got home, she was sick, you know, really sick, with vomiting and all that stuff, she wouldn't be complaining about it. Do you see what I'm saying?

She's not somebody who's always complaining or trying to get things for herself.

She's not all wrapped up in her own little world, thinking just about herself.

When I was a kid, there wasn't anything she wouldn't do for me. You know, we didn't have a lot of things but she would make up games that we would play. Or, let's say we were going to go to the beach. She would take a couple of pil-low cases and she would dunk them in the water and then flap them up and down to fill them with air and tie the open end of each pillow case with a string and then tie the strings to-gether. She'd make them into pontoons so that I could float.

Well, of course they didn't really work, but she was always trying to something.

She was always trying to make things be good.

Even for my father, although he was never happy. He was always yelling at her about one thing or another and at me about everything. I always knew that one or the other of us was going to get it. He didn't use to hit her, though. He just yelled at her and talked to her like she was dumb. He was never satisfied. Never.

He made it hard. When I turned about eight, he thought I was too old to spank. That's when he started using his fist. How could I stand up to him? And what was she supposed to do? He would keep at her, badgering and bullying with his big voice and his logic until she'd be in tears. I didn't know how to help her. Even the two of us together was just no match for him.

But, do you see what I'm saying? She never complained. She just kept trying to make everything good.

★★★★★★★★★★★★★★★

I have let my jaw go slack with my mouth open in a sleeping pose.

"Edmund!" fat Miriam calls.

I don't move.

"Edmund, come on! Time to rouse! Edmund!"

She takes a hold of my foot and begins moving it back and forth, wiggling it.

"Come on, Edmund." she says.

I open my eyes slowly, not to give up my game too willingly because the next time she might believe. If I get caught trying to trick her she will always use it as an excuse to do what she pleases. I can hear her.

"You can't trust that old Edmund. He'll try anything!

And every time, too!" she says.

I don't want to give her any ammunition so I pretend to awaken slowly and then close my eyes as though I am beginning to doze again.

"Oh no you don't," she says. "C'mon, Edmund. C'mon, time to rise and shine."

My diaper is damp from the perspiration around my waist and from the perspiration that my genitals generate. Today I did not wet my bed. When I do, it irritates the other nurses. Oh, my God, such a childish thing to do. Of course, they are not the ones trying to hold back for two or three hours, bloated and uncomfortable, not being understood when looked in upon, unable to make the communication about a need. I try sometimes, to point to my diaper or my cock, but they don't understand.

They don't really care whether I pee in my bed. The issue is that if my sheets are wet the nurses have to change them. Not an easy chore, I don't suppose, rolling me over to my side, stuffing half of the sheet that is already on the bed underneath my side, putting the new sheet along the vacant side of the mattress, tucking it in, drawing it across to the other, dirty sheet and pushing it snugly against my side, then rolling me over the other way and completing the process by pulling the old sheet off the bed and pulling the new sheet across the mattress and tucking it in.

On the other hand, the option is to get another nurse in the room, pull me up by my shoulders, which sometimes ache, tie the wide, webbed belt around my mid-section, rotate my legs off the bed, stand me up, tum me around, sit me in the wheel chair and take me to the bathroom. In the bathroom I have to be assisted out of the chair and onto the toilet seat where they hold me, balancing me, so I can either urinate or defecate. Or both! Sometimes I hit the jackpot and everybody is happy.

At first it was very embarrassing to me to be found lying in bed with no covers over me and my hospital gown hiked up above my stomach, my genitals exposed. And sometimes with an erection. Especially in the mornings. I would try to cover myself with my hands. If it were Miriam, the big, fat bitch, who happened to be the nurse I was trying to hide myself from she would always have some kind of a remark to make.

She says, "Now, Edmund, it's nothing I haven't seen before.[11]

As though I care what she has or hasn't seen before. But the way she says it really makes me wonder if it is something she sees other than in this nursing home.

This morning was a bad start.

When Miriam came in and when I had finished my game of pretending to sleep, I realized that I was uncovered. Like I said, I used to be embarrassed if I were found that way. I no longer am, though. Not with Miriam. I don't care enough about the bitch to be embarrassed. I just don't want her to see me. She doesn't see me as a person. To her I'm just another piece of shit that she has to care for in her lousy, dirty, boring, under-paid job at the nursing home. She's told me.

And there she is. There's Miriam, standing at the foot of my bed, watching while I tried to get my hands positioned over my cock. If I try to put my hand on my nose it's as likely to end up on my cheek as it is my forehead or my chin or my mouth.

She stood there and watched me fumbling away with my hands. I would get a hand down on my side and work it over to my stomach and then try to push it down to my cock. But, as luck would have it, it ended up on my thigh and I had to try to work it over from there.

"C'mon big boy, quit trying to play with yourself," she said. "You have better things to do. And I have better things to do than sit here and watch you and get myself all excited just by seeing your size." And then she gives me this smile and a wink. "You know how it is, Edmund, you old lover-boy. If you get me excited then I might do something crazy like, well I don't know exactly, now, do I.

"So, let's get you up and into the bathroom and then breakfast and into the hall for a visit with your friends. I'll bet Mr. Durkin will stop by to talk with you. Doesn't he usually stop by and the two of you have a little chat in the hall? Do the two of you have a meeting of the minds?" and then she laughs her forced, staccato, chirping laugh.

Mr. Durkin. James is his first name, I think. He wanders the hallways, always with his rubber-tipped wooden cane in hand, talking non-stop. He's senile. The old tape recordings spew out. Old man Durkin is usually telling me how, in some fashion or another, I had better learn to behave myself. Or else!

"You enjoy your visits with Mr. Durkin, don't you," Miriam said.

I looked at her. She stood at the foot of my bed.

"C'mon sweetie," she said, "you do now, don't you?"

I told her to go fuck herself but she didn't understand me.

She sang my name. "Edmund." Her hands went to her hips. "I surely do wish you could talk. Shame on you, silly.[11]

Then she laughed and reached out, giving my calf a squeeze with her hand.

If I could have made a muscle in my leg I would have. She hurt me and all I could do was move my leg. I have no muscles.

Wait a minute. I shouldn't say that. I have to have some muscles or else I couldn't move my arms at all and I could never get to my other side in the bed. Right?

The atrophy started before I came here. I was in McCann General Hospital for the longest damn time. Six months. They worked me as well as they could, I guess, and then they decided that I couldn't make any progress.

The atrophy makes me hurt. You wouldn't think that a squeeze from some bitch-nurse like Miriam Samuelson could make me hurt. But there isn't any muscle wrapped around the bone anymore. There is flesh. Loose flesh. Without the muscle the flesh seems more tender. It hurts more easily if you get bumped. Or squeezed too hard.

At McCann Hospital, they would take me to the physical therapy section. I would be strapped in the wheelchair. Already, the muscles in my legs and back were too weak to allow me to sit upright.

The rubber wheels on the chair would glide smoothly across the polished grey tile floor which was bordered on either side, next to the walls, in black.

I remember those hallways.

They would wheel me to the elevators in the Levine section. The trip through the hallways was the best part of the therapy. There were people in the halls. Sometimes they moved in gusts of white nurses' uniforms, billowing like spinnakers.

Occasionally there would be faces that I recognized. I'm not talking about the nurses or doctors that were always in the hospital. I'm talking about people from another time in my life.

Once, I saw a teacher from the high school. It was Mr. Berry. He recognized me too, I'm sure. My head was all tilted to one side like it is when I'm in the wheelchair in this place, but our eyes met. I saw the recognition with him. He didn't nod or wave or anything, but he knew that he knew me from somewhere. We used to call Mr. Berry, "Dingle."

It's in the eyes. The eyes don't change. You can cut your face up and you can have a stroke or get real fat or make any kind of change like that but you can't change those eyes. That's how you can tell if you know someone. The eyes. The eye contact. A lot of things change. Like with me. I'm not so big anymore. Not like I was before my stroke. If I had had friends, say, before my stroke, which I didn't, really, and they came to see me now they might say, if they were being honest, "Man, have you ever changed." Of course, I've changed. But they would still recognize me when they looked into my eyes. A lot of other things are different now, maybe everything, you might say, except the eyes. They're the same.

I'm not big anymore, I'm little. For Chrisake, I mean I've probably lost about eighty pounds. Jesus! Think about it. I guess that makes me about one hundred and thirty pounds now. If I could stand up and look at myself in the mirror, I'd probably faint.

Anyway, these friends of mine, I don't know what they might be thinking because what somebody might be thinking is not what they are saying. Unless, of course, it happens to be that you're talking to someone you trust. Like Tammy. I mean, it's obvious that I could tell her anything. Or just about anything, anyway. And I think it's true for her, too. I mean, I think she could tell me anything. I'm sure she could and I'd still feel the same as before about her. I can't remember what they call that. It's that whatever kind of love. Or in our case, that whatever kind of friendship because we don't have love, really. It's friendship. Right?

The therapists at the hospital tried helping me to crawl again. Like a child. They tried to get me to walk while there was a physical therapist on either side of me and a walker in hand. I was able to put some pressure on the walker with my hands. Squeezing. I think I can remember feeling my nails bite into the heel of my hand while I squeezed that chrome tubing. Maybe they did.

But my arms, they were funny. They were busy going all over the place. They pivoted in my shoulder, and caused my elbows, which were bent, to make these crazy, uncontrolled arcs. This black nurse was passing from the opposite direction one day.

"Well, look at him now, will you?" she said. "That boy ain't got no rhythm at all. Ain't got none!"

Then she laughed, her voice getting swallowed up by the insulation of the wrapped pipes overhead and the acoustical ceiling. It was pretty funny to me and I laughed inside. I grinned too, and then saliva spilled over my lip and down my chin like it does.

There were two therapists and they would hang onto the thick belt. I would try to walk. Thonest to God I would try! But my dumb fucking legs wouldn't move right. I couldn't raise one foot and put it in front of the other. My big fucking feet were as though they were in thick, sucking mud. They weren't going anywhere no matter how hard I tried to get them moving. They just wouldn't lift off of the floor.

They tried having a third therapist, one wearing knee pads, crawl behind me on his knees, holding onto each of my ankles with each of his hands. They were trying to get my brain to relay the messages to my body, to bring back some memory of walking, but they couldn't help me. My brain knew what was going on. I could hear the therapist's talking. I processed the information. My body just wouldn't respond. My legs just wouldn't do what I tried so hard to get them to do. They wouldn't do that thing that I could never remember not being able to do.

"Move, you fucker," I used to say to my leg. "C'mon, God-damnit, you no good son of-a-bitch."

★★★★★★★★★★★★★★★

Miriam says, "Okay, let's go. Let's face the day. Come on Edmund. If I can, then so can you."

She pulls the sheet down to the foot of the bed. As often happens, my adult diaper has come off during the night. It's lying under one cheek of my ass. I'm dry, too. I can see her checking me out to see if I have a hard-on. I don't, which I am thankful for this morning because I'm not in any mood to be talked to by her about it. I'm over-tired from all of the talking and the staying-awake-stuff with you. It's tiring. I'm not trying to be irrelevant or anything like that, but it seems to take a terrific amount of concentration for me to make each new sentence. And then I think, well, if I'm going to go through the effort to do this and if I'm really going to trust you, Tammy, then I might as well try.

I don't mean faking to be honest. What I mean is, really being honest. That's what I'm talking about. I'm not talking about some kind of game that I'll play with you to occupy my time or waste yours. That's what it would be if I weren't being honest. It would mean that all the effort, caring and writing that you have invested would be negated. And that would be pretty stupid for me to be doing at this point. Here I am. I've nowhere left to go. And even if all of this talking doesn't help me, it might not hurt me. And even if it does hurt, so what? Is there a difference anyway?

And that's a strange way for me to feel. Well, maybe not strange, but different. Most of my life has been a matter of getting through from one point to the next rather than having to worry about trying to do a good job or consciously making an effort to do the best that I can at any given time.

Ironic. That probably describes it the best. Now that there isn't much left of my body, my mind finally begins to function in a less cluttered way. Not perfect, of course, but less cluttered and less confused in certain ways. Sometimes, as I lie here in the bed or as I sit out in the hallway, I have a sense of being at one with myself instead of being continually fractured or broken apart. Sometimes I feel as though I could be normal even as I realize that I can't do the things with my body that, inf act, would show the world that I am normal.

The major thing, I suppose, is that I can't get the God-damned words out in such a way that I can be understood. That communication thing is a barrier. The biggest barrier. If I could talk then someone else could listen. If I could talk then I could relay or verbalize ideas, thoughts, feelings. You know what it is that I'm saying. I could make known what might be happening with me. Maybe, of course, say, just like anybody else, I might be having a problem with some confusion about one thing or another just like we all do.

Don't we? Maybe in my case the problem, or the confusion just gets magnified a little. Or maybe even sometimes it gets magnified a lot. So what? What's the difference? You see, the thing is, I can even know that something is not right with me and still not be able to do anything about it because there isn't anything that I can do to communicate it.

Jesus, what a world of the mind.

Just to be out in the night when the moon starts to come up out of nowhere over the horizon of the water. To stand on the shore, even alone. To feel the summer. Just to be there with the moon, watching it while the gulls circle overhead.

Or hear the bus driver call out the next stop.

What am I left with, anyway? How long have I been sitting in the hall? Have I been waiting for the next meal for ten minutes or twelve? For twelve minutes or two hours?

How many tiles in the floor? How many passes will Richard, the maintenance man make with his push broom when he sweeps the floor? Will he look in tomorrow as he passes my door?

He didn't today.

★★★★★★★★★★★★★★★

Miriam looks at me. "I'm going to get some help."

I want to tell her not to bother, that I think I'll just lay in bed and take it easy this morning. Fat chance.

She stops at the door well and looks back at me. "Now, Edmund," she says, and she's got this particular look on her face with her head cocked to one side, a crooked little smile on her lips, "don't you be playing with yourself while I'm gone."

When she walks out I can hear her thighs rubbing together. It's a scratching sound, probably high up on her legs where her white nurse's hose ends. One fat thigh rubbing against the other, making the nylon scratch back and forth with each step. Scratching up near where it's warm.

Shit. She could offer it up to me on a silver platter and I could care less. And it's not that I don't have any sex-drive left. Otherwise, why would I wake up with a hard-on almost every morning?

I turn my head and try to look out of the tall, narrow windows on the west wall. I see that the sky is gray this morning. I roll a little more onto my left side, but not all of the way.

Sometimes in the evening the way the sun is setting can make for a sky that's maybe like a Montana sky. Pinks and blues and clouds that look orange. Clouds that sometimes look like they might catch on fire, or already are. It makes me think of how the sky probably looks when you're out on the plains. Someplace where there aren't any buildings, maybe not even a forest.

Then I think about Indians sitting on their horses.

I think I could have been a good Indian. Maybe I would have been the kind that could hunt and run for miles without needing water. I probably could have speared some fish in the creek that runs by our campsite and taken them to the tepee where my squaw would fix them for dinner while I played with our youngsters.

They never cried. Did you know that? And if one of them was different than the others, nobody made fun. It was okay.

When I'm standing, they rotate me slowly until my back is to the wheelchair and then shuffle me back a foot or so and that's when old fat-ass says, "Now." They start to ease the pressure of their lift and my legs begin to collapse. If the wheels of the chair aren't locked and I'm not far enough back into the seat, I might end up on the floor. If my butt only catches the edge of the seat then the chair rolls away from me, I might drop onto the tile floor. It's happened before and it hurts like hell.

"Wait!" Anna says. "The wheels! Lock the wheels, Miriam!"

Miriam and Anna hold me where I am and Miriam reaches down with one hand and balances me with the other and pulls the brake lever forward.

"Good catch, Anna," she says, and she gives her a smile. "Thanks," she says.

"Glad to help, dear," Anna said.

Miriam goes to my dresser, takes my slippers and puts them on my feet. She owers the footrests but scrapes my ankle bone on it. It bums.

Fuck you!

"You're welcome," she says. Then she looks to Anna and says, "You know, Edmund is one of the best. I love it when he thanks me." She looks back at me. "Aren't we special to each other, Edmund?"

I tum my head and look away.

"Anna, I am making him blush," she says, and laughs. Then the bitch pinches my cheek like I'm some fucking three-year-old.

They wheel me into the bathroom so that they can stand me up and tum me and then seat me on the toilet.

I start pushing with my stomach muscles, gently at first and then harder. It's not too difficult to get my bowels started. I'm grateful. I felt good at that moment. Successful.

Fifteen minutes later I was dressed. I was going someplace. To the hallway. The corridor. You know, the passageway right outside the door to my room. Big fucking deal.

And also, stupid-ass Miriam doesn't secure the webbed belt tightly enough to keep me secure in the chair. She leaves it too God-damned loose.

★★★★★★★★★★★★★★★

I could hear the clanking of the trays on the carts that are wheeled out from the kitchen by one of the cooks. Maybe the food here is good compared to other places like this.

Maybe they're really more like fine French chefs for all I know. The thing is, I'll never find out.

Fat Miriam comes and wheels me out into the hall. I sit in the rear, the furthest from the nurse's station.

In front of me is Rosemary. She was in front of me from the first day that they put me out here. I've never heard any of the nurses use her last name. She's just plain old Rosemary.

The first couple of days that I was sitting behind her made me uncomfortable. She has thin, pure white hair. Some of it wants to curl, like maybe it's trying to cover the pink skin of her scalp. She's shriveled. She couldn't have been this small when she was younger. I mean, she's not a dwarf or a midget, you know? She's just tiny. I can hear her talk when the nurses ask her something. Her voice comes from somewhere very close to her mouth. It's from high up in her throat and it cracks.

Rosemary's arms are very skinny and her hands are bony as hell with a whole bunch of blue veins sticking out on the back of her hands and along her arms. And her hands, besides all of these God-damn blue veins, have these large, brown, aging spots. As big as dimes.

Skinny as she is, she still has that old loose-flesh thing that old people have. Skinny old people have all kinds of loose flesh hanging around. And wrinkles, too. They have more wrinkles than the fat ones. The skinny ones remind me of baby birds with necks that are trying to hold up something that looks to be too heavy. And when they turn their heads they all seem to have these Adam's apples jutting out.

All five of us, the ones in the wheelchairs are now sitting in the hall. The food has been taken into the room where they feed us. They start wheeling us down the hall, past the nurse's station and into what is our dining room. Some of the wheelchair contingent is able to manage eating on their own. Then there are the rest of us, three of us if you want to know, who have to be fed by the nurses. Betsy, one of the nurses wheels me into the room and I sit facing the large windows that look out onto the curved driveway that leads to the main entrance.

Sometimes, it's a pretty nice to see cars coming around the driveway to drop someone off who lives in one of the other wings, or maybe to pick them up. It's a break in the day. It's nicer still when the sun is shining and the trees have leaves and when the grass is green on the lawn beyond the driveway. Sometimes, on a winter day when I know that it is cold as hell outside, I can feel kind of good about being in the room, looking out, not having to freeze my ass off just to get to work. I would especially not like having to get to this place. I mean, of course we'd all die if the people didn't make it here, but really, it does seem like it might be kind of depressing to be around all of us five days a week. I said might be?

Jesus! It would be. No question in my mind, but I swear to God we'd trade places with you in a minute. At least I know I would.

Miriam sits down next to me and puts my tray on the table.

Eating isn't much fun. Not like it used to be. Now I have to be fed each bite. If I'm not hungry, then I keep my mouth closed and they get the message. Even fat Miriam gets the message.

Miriam has this evil about her.

Sometimes, like I said before, she'll squeeze my leg too hard. She digs her fingers into my calf, probing.

She has more tricks, too. Sometimes when she puts me back to bed, she'll get me too far toward the head of the bed and so when she turns me and gets my legs up on the bed and lowers me down, my head will hit the metal frame of the rails in the headboard. That doesn't happen when anyone else puts me down. It's no accident.

She's got a whole bag of tricks, that bitch does. Are you surprised?

If she's having a really shitty day, she sits me up in the bed by pulling my hair with one hand and pulling on the back of my head with the other. I mean, it feels like somebody is putting a hot iron rod down the top of my spine. And I know she does it on purpose because before she does one of these little numbers on me, she always looks over her shoulder to see if another patient happens to be standing at the door looking in, or if there might a nurse passing by who might see something she wouldn't want her to see.

Understand?

Sometimes when she's feeding me, she'll pull the fork out of my mouth and scrape the roof of my mouth with the talons.

Who's going to find out?

Still, we're kind of even I suppose. She knows that I think she's a fuck, and I know that she doesn't like me.

★★★★★★★★★★★★★★★

After breakfast Miriam leaves me parked along the wall next to the door of my room.

The other sitters are lined up along the wall too.

There are occasions when somebody in our group will say something strange to one of the other people or maybe just to themselves. You know, talking out of their head. Maybe they didn't get what they usually get for their medication. I say that about their medication because when it happens that somebody starts in just blabbing away, one of the nurses will often bring a pill and the little paper cup of water and down the hatch it goes. About ten minutes after the pill is popped, I'll be able to see their head nodding down to their chest and then jerking up, just like I used to do when I would be sitting at my desk in school but too tired to stay awake. Their head might nod like that for a few minutes and then on one of the nods it will stay down for fifteen or twenty minutes while they have a cat nap.

Sometimes the same thing happens to me without me getting any medication. I'll be sitting there just feeling so damned drowsy that my head will begin to nod. I might try to get my elbow positioned on the armrest so that then, with luck, I might be able to rest my chin, or the side of my face on my hand, but usually by then I'm just too tired to try.

Sometimes it's just too much of an effort. This morning I was in that tired state. Probably from all of that talking and staying awake that I did last night. I'm not saying that it's your fault, but that probably is why. I was just over-tired from us doing that talking last night.

Anyway, I was sitting there, being sleepy but not being able to ask that fat Miriam to get me to bed when, honest to Christ, around the corner next to the nurse's station comes my father. It *was* my father. I swear to God. And he had the cane that he used to use when he took his walks around the block.

He started coming down the hallway toward me. He was trying to camouflage what he was doing by pretending to visit with the other people as he came. He was acting like this real friendly guy who was here just to cheer all of us up. But all the time while he was making his way down the hall, I knew he was going to get me. He had me trapped!

It was him in the flesh. It wasn't like I was a little kid again. Nothing like that. This time I was an adult and here, in the nursing home, right in the hall. He was making his way, trying not to attract too much attention as he came. He had a plan.

When he would get to me, he would beat the shit out of me with the cane and what was I supposed to do? I couldn't yell for help. All I could do was try to attract somebody's attention by making a lot of noise which I started doing. I was trying to yell words but of course they were just coming out like noises to whoever might hear them.

He was getting closer and nobody was paying attention. I kept trying to yell and I was trying to wave to the nurse at the station but she was sitting down at the desk and all I could see of her was her cap and the phone at her ear.

Jesus Christ!

He was practically on top of me!

My arms were flapping around and I started trying to raise my feet off the footrests so that I could try to push them against the floor to get me out of there. If I could get my feet on the floor I could back up. I could push hard and propel myself backwards down the hall and away from him. But I couldn't get my feet off the footrests. Then I tried to pitch myself forward, thinking that maybe I could get the chair rolling forward. It didn't go anywhere. I pushed myself against the back of the chair, fast, and then forward again because that fucker was close now and he had the cane raised up and I knew he was going to brain me and all I wanted to do was to get my head out of the way.

The belt that holds me was loose, thanks to fat-ass-Miriam and when I went forward the last time I just kept going. I was so far forward by the time the belt grabbed at my ribs and stomach that my momentum just kept taking me forward and then the rear wheels came off the floor and followed me. I pitched forward and couldn't get my fucking arms to work to help to break my fall.

I landed on my forehead.

I was on the floor and I was trapped with that fucking wheelchair on top of me, and then I could hear people yelling. There was commotion. People were yelling from up and down the hall. I heard the nurses' feet on the floor while they were running toward me and I could tell that I was bleeding badly because my eye that was close to the floor was filling with blood. I was hoping that I was cut on the outside and that I wasn't bleeding from the brain. Then I thought that maybe I was going to die and there was nothing I could do about it, so I just lay still.

The longer I lay there, the more it seemed okay to be hurt as long as I wasn't going to be bashed on the skull with the cane. And I knew that he would never bash me on the head with all of those people around. I was glad the nurses were there. I didn't even mind fat Miriam right then.

When they got me up, they put a cloth on my forehead and then about two seconds later another nurse brought an ice pack and they put that against my forehead.

They wheeled me into my room and laid me on my back and raised the back of the bed some and they all really treated me nice.

They were all talking at me, speculating about what had happened and had I had a stroke and should they look at my history to see if I'm epileptic. And then somebody says that they bet that I am and so on and so forth and then after a while, the doctor comes.

"Hello, Edmund, I'm Dr. Gitzman. Do you remember me?" he says. I try to nod a little.

"Good," he says. "Quite a fall you took."

He put a cover over my face; it was claustrophobic. He gave me some shots of Novocain and they burned and then he spent some time sewing me up. I don't know how many stitches he put in, and I don't know how long it took.

When he finished, Miriam tied each of my wrists with a cloth and tied the cloths to the siderail. I guess she did it so I wouldn't accidentally pull an arm up and hit myself in the forehead. That was okay.

Actually, the whole thing worked out pretty well because later they let me sleep and not be bothered.

★★★★★★★★★★★★★★★★

I slept until the dinner hour and I wasn't hungry when I woke. Edith was untying the knots from one of my wrists. My other hand was already free.

Edith was in and out of my room. She treated me nicely, asking if my head hurt and did I feel nauseated. I didn't. I guess they might have thought that I had a concussion. I always thought you weren't supposed to let anyone sleep if they might have a concussion. At least not right away. It would have been kind of ironic, don't you think? You know, me, ending up dying from a fall out of a chair because I thought I was going to be beaten by a dead man.

Of course, now I know what happened.

It was old man Durkin who came down the hall pointing at people and talking to everybody like he does. I saw him getting closer and closer and I swear to God that he was my father to me. Don't ask me how, but right at that time he was.

The rest of the night passed quietly for me. Edith didn't give me any trouble at all and she and the Thornton woman, who is it, Helen? They were gentle when they took me to the bathroom. It was nice.

They gave me a bath. You know, a sponge bath. But it wasn't the usual slop-the water-over-his-body-quick kind of sponge bath. The bath was all over, and they took their time and the washcloths felt good with the warm water and soap. They washed my feet and between my toes and both sides of me, front and back. Nice, almost worth the fall.

Outside, when I turned my head to look, I could see that there was a nice kind of glow as the evening turned to night. I could tell that it was going to be a nice, light night and that maybe the moon was going to be full and that there were not any clouds in the sky. The moon comes up from the east somewhere. I used to see it rise over the lake and be so huge and gold. The horizon made it look larger; I think. I used to hold my thumb and forefinger at arm's length and then I would make a space between them and fit the moon into the space. And when the moon was high off the horizon, I would do the same thing and it would seem to be the same space.

It's like, the moon climbs into the sky every night. Right? We just can't always see it.

But if we had the right perspective we could see it, couldn't we? I mean, it's there.

We live with the presence and we live with the absence. But the absence is really our own perception of void. The void is our own absence of perception. We know of the mass and the volume and location. We know of the existence and the arc and the velocity. We talk of the part of; the quarter, the half, the three-quarter.

We only talk from what it is that we choose to acknowledge and we don't acknowledge what we know is there but that we don't see. And the strange thing is, somewhere, we know that we don't acknowledge what in fact we know is there. What is. What is the real of reality.

Tammy?

You can talk now, Tammy, I'm finished.

★★★★★★★★★★★★★★★★

She looked up at me and laid her pencil down. She sat for a bit before she spoke.

"You've had a day, Edmund, with that fall, and all," she said.

Yeah, I guess so. More than my regular day, I suppose. But still, not a terrible day, really.

"Not a terrible day?" she said. No, not really.

We stayed quiet for a minute or two.

"If today wasn't a terrible day, what would you say was?" she said.

Oh, Jesus, I don't know. I guess I've had some terrible days. I mean, each day that I had a breakdown was probably a terrible day. But of course, I don't remember much of those days. All of a sudden, I would find myself in the hospital and I might have been there for a week or two before I became aware of anything like my surroundings.

"How about the day you had your heat stroke. Was that a terrible day?" she said.

Well, it must have been, but I don't remember anything about it. I was working, you know. I was on the job helping to deliver appliances and I guess that I went into a coma and then the paramedics came and took me to the hospital. But I don't remember it, so it's hard for me to say that I had a terrible day that day. I mean, of course I can look at my situation now and know that it was really a rotten fucking day. Of course, it had to be the worst fucking day in my life. Look at the results. I mean, I can't think that it wasn't the worst day of my life twenty times over. Look at how full of shit my life is now.

But in other ways, I'm probably healthier than I was before. Of course, I'm not perfect and I hallucinate, like this morning, but I think that happens because I just get too bored.

Wheelchair to bed and back again and then to the bed again. Nobody to talk to, except you. Everything always just going on in my head.

What else do I have to do with my life now except think about it and explore myself and my life and try to understand it? I can't read because my eyes wander all over the fucking place. I can't talk to anybody except you. I can't go to the bathroom whenever I might feel like it. I can't go for a walk or feed myself or comb my own hair. I mean, for Christ-sake,

I can't even jag-off if I want. All I have is to think and sort, think and sort.

"Do you remember when you had your last breakdown?" she said.

I had to think for a minute.

Yeah, it was after my father died.

"Oh, really?" she said. "Were the two things connected?"

Jesus, Tammy. Everything that has ever happened to us is connected, isn't it? I mean, how could it be otherwise?

"Oh, of course," she says.

We look at each other.

"Would you tell me about your father? I mean, his dying?" she says.

I don't know if I have the energy. Let me think for a minute.

I rested and then took a deep breath.

Okay, I'll tell you what I remember about it.

★★★★★★★★★★★★★★★

I was working as a mail clerk. An office boy. I was running errands and doing whatever else was in need of doing.

When I found out that my father was sick, I went to Mitchell's office to tell him.

Mitchell Steiner was his name.

I had only been working there for a few months when I had to tell him about my father.

Mitchell, I said, my father is dying. I called him by his first name because he had told me to. That was pretty nice for me. It made me comfortable with him.

He leaned back in his leather chair on the other side of the desk and lowered his glasses on his nose, looking over them. Mitchell was seventy-one with thin white hair combed back. He was short with these real powerful arms that had made him a good puncher when he was young and in the Navy. He had been the champion boxer in his weight class at the base where he was stationed.

Now he was the owner of an office supply company. A small company. Three stores, I think. Mitchell always referred to it as small but it seemed pretty big to me. We were always busy. One of the stores was right below us, on the first floor of the building where our offices were.

It was kind of like Mitchell saved me.

You know how it is on the applications where they ask you to tell what you've been doing with your time in a chronological way? Well, none of the companies was willing to hire me. There were big gaps of time that weren't accounted for. What was I supposed to do, put down, "Oops, another breakdown?"

Well, Mitchell hired me. He was willing. I had only been working there for a few months when I had to tell him about my father. I didn't like to have to do that because Mitchell had given me a chance and now, I felt I was going to be letting him down even though I remembered what he told me when he hired me.

He said, "This is more than a business, Edmund. It's family. That's what the company is. It's family."

That's what he said. He said he trusted me. He said that he thought I would fit in just fine. Those were his words. "Just fine."

I tried to look directly at Mitchell. He has cancer, I said.

He spoke with this soft voice that he had, and slowly, as he always did. He was deliberate with his words.

"I'm sorry, Edmund," he said.

It's a progressive sort of thing and they can't stop it. Most likely, I'm going to have to miss some work, I said.

He tilted forward and stood, reaching his hand across the desk to me. I took his hand to shake but he put his other hand out and stood there, holding my hand with both of his. His hands were large and warm.

"Edmund," he said, "of course. You take whatever time you need." He rubbed my hand some while he held it and talked.

"If there is anything I can do," he said. And he meant it. He looked at me in his easy way.

I had to get to the hospital. I had to hop the train and get to the apartment so that I could get up to the hospital.

I wasn't doing too well. I was getting so damned tired that sometimes I would fall asleep on the train and miss my stop and then I would have to take another train back for one or two stops or else walk. Sometimes I walked even though I knew it would be faster to be going back on the train. But the thing is, I wasn't feeling too good generally and the fresh air seemed to make me a little less sick. I had been throwing up a lot.

At the hospital there were tubes.

Plenty of tubes and lines and bottles and bags and a particularly strong, sharp smell of urine.

My father was in the hospital and lay in the bed, dying. I didn't tell him that he was, and I don't think any of the doctor's had told him either. The doctors were always trying to fix the last thing that had complicated a complicated situation even more.

Or, maybe the continued complications were keeping the dogs of death at bay. Death was barking right outside the open door but I was able to concern myself with the latest platelet count and ask, "How is his blood pressure now? Nurse? How is it? Okay?"

She would look over at me. [11]It's fine," she would say.

But it didn't matter. Not the urgency of the next ten minutes or the agony of the next ten days. He wasn't getting better. Never would. He had had his time and now he was dying. Cancer.

The room that he was in carried a smell that was stronger by the day, if not, at times by the hour. As I approached from the corridor, the door ajar, the odor drifting into the hall made my body work at odds with itself. My legs would continue towards my father while my chest and arms wanted to heave backwards away from the room with its large heavy grey door.

Inside was my father, sallow, drawn, lying in the bed with the tubes. Lines of plastic tubing into his nostrils to help supply oxygen, a plastic bag with glucose, dripping intravenously, supplying liquid sugar, a catheter in his penis for the urine which flowed into the plastic bag slung on the lower side rail of the bed and a tube into his mouth to evacuate the mucus build-up in his lungs. Sometimes, there was another bag hung above the bed which was plasma transfusing into a vein in his leg. The smell and the hum of the equipment and his labored breathing was always present.

My father had been in the hospital for three months.

During the two weeks preceding his death there was no more about the new marketing scheme, or the new idea for importing some fantastic product that he didn't know the name of but was sure was out there.

In lieu of the fantasies about becoming successful, he became quieter and his skin yellowed more.

Standing next to his side, or sitting in one of the chairs next to his bed, I would wait for what was going to happen eventually. When I stood next to him, I would tire in my concentration, trying to distinguish if he was laboring with his breathing or if the vacuum was making the rasping sound as it evacuated the liquid from his lungs.

After a while I would take one of the extra pans that was always there and with cool water and a washcloth, I would bathe his face. Also, the top of his head. He would look peaceful after I had done this. Then I would do his hands. I would wash each finger and the palm. Then I would bathe his feet, each toe and the arch, giving a gentle massage.

When I would finish, a faint smile would cross his lips.

And the last night he was alive, after the washcloth routine, he said, "Thank you." There was something more that I wanted him to say, so I nudged the bed. Just a little. He said, "What do you want now?"

Back then I still held onto the idea that maybe he really loved me. I couldn't imagine that he didn't.

He wouldn't have had to say the words. That can be a hard thing to do. I know that.

He could have given me a hug sometimes when I was a kid. That would have been enough to have made me sure that he did. He wouldn't have had to say anything. He could have just given me a hug. I would have known what it meant.

Since he had been sick, I had told him a couple of times that I loved him. I was hoping.

I never told him that I hated him, but I guess I did that too, years before..

I don't even remember the reasons that he used to hit me. I never really knew what it was that I had done wrong. And then when I did do something wrong, like the time I was caught trying to steal some money from my seventh-grade teacher's purse, he didn't do anything to me. He laughed, as though I had almost gotten away with a very clever thing.

And I helped him, too. I kept him from getting in trouble. One of my teacher's, Mrs. Turner, it was fifth grade, asked me about some marks on my face. "What happened?" she said. She sat behind her desk, her hands resting on a closed book. She waited for my response. I didn't have much of an answer. I told her I didn't know. I didn't know what to say really, but I knew that I couldn't tell her.

I thought my father and I had some kind of a deal worked out between us. He could do what he wanted to me and I would never tell teachers or friends or anybody and I would be afraid of him and I would hate him. My payoff would be that someday he would tell me that it had just all been a test and that he really did love me. The trouble was, he forgot to keep his end of the bargain.

Mitchell came to his funeral. I don't remember if I called work to tell anyone. I think not. But they came, five or six of them, and Mitchell. And I was glad that he was there when he held my hand and I couldn't speak. I remember that I was happy to see that he spoke to my mother. I stood and nodded.

Maybe three days later, I don't remember exactly, I was back on the train, on my way to work. It was odd. I had this urge to yell, to shout to all the people in the car that my father had just died a few days ago and what were they doing acting like nothing at all had happened. Instead, pages of the newspapers were turned and read and glanced at and turned again and one station followed another while we headed toward the core.

The receptionist nodded when I went in the office. There were some other looks and nods. Quiet acknowledgements.

On the way down the hall to the mail desk, I passed Mitchell's office.

The door was open and he was sitting on the leather couch, looking at me across the large expanse of space. He motioned for me to come in, reaching his arms out.

I remember.

I heard the heavy teakwood door close quietly with a click behind me.

The air in the room was very still. And hot. And it was humid, too. I breathed deeply and began to reach for my collar, to loosen my tie and undo the button. My shirt collar felt so tight around my neck. I felt like I couldn't breathe very well. And Mitchell sat, looking so awfully far away. My jacket was heavy, weighing across my shoulders and clinging to my back. And my forehead was damp. I needed to wipe my forehead.

I took two or three small steps, then I sagged and went down, crawling, groping, as it were, slowly, along the soft thick carpet. I saw the wool pile between my fingers as they curled and clenched.

★★★★★★★★★★★★★★★

"God, so difficult, your father dying and all. So painful," she said.

Yeah, I suppose it was. I mean, of course it was. It was enough that I couldn't deal with it. And that led me to be here, really. The fucking medicine that they gave me after that breakdown and when I had that next job delivering appliances, helped me have the heat stroke.

Tammy sits and looks at me. She doesn't say anything and neither do I. We're not staring each other down, we're just there, each looking at the other.

I need some water.

She smiled and went into the bathroom and drew water into the pitcher that's kept in my room.

I watched her walk the few steps toward the bathroom. Her legs look nice. Very nice.

She has slim ankles and then her legs taper upwards, widening gently. Her calf muscle shows just below the hem of her white nurse's dress.

"I thought we were talking about your father's death. How it was for you. Would you like some ice, Edmund?" she says.

No. No thanks. So, we were. Does that mean I don't see other things?

She poured some water into my glass and took the straw and put it to my lips. I sucked the water down in two gulps.

My head felt tender high up on my forehead. It was throbbing a little. "Would you like a pain pill?" she said.

No, not really. Maybe later if it gets worse. And then we sat for a few minutes.

You look kind of sexy tonight, Miss Rothchild. I laughed quietly.

What? Blushing? Do I see a little blush coming out around those nice, prominent, high-set cheekbones? Is that a blush that I see? Or am I imagining because of this bump on my forehead?

"Edmund, where is this coming from?" she said. What do you mean?

"This morning when I said goodbye and kissed you on the forehead you started reacting and telling me that I don't like you in that way. You told me not to do that and now you're lying there making comments about my being attractive. Sexual kinds of comments," she said. "And yes, I blushed. Why wouldn't I?"

Okay, okay. I'm sorry. I shouldn't have said anything like that. I just felt like teasing you a little.

"Is that all it was? Just teasing?" she said.

Well, kind of. I mean, yeah, it was teasing. But it wasn't, "Just teasing." It was true, too.

"Well, then I guess you are saying that you find me to be attractive also, even though you think I'm somewhat over-weight. Right, Edmund?" she said.

I didn't say you were overweight.

"Yes, you did, Edmund. Last night, when we first began you said that I was, this big lady, and you said that you didn't find me appealing. And also, to refresh your memory, you said that I was about twice your age. I mean, please!" she said.

No, I didn't. I never said that about you.

"Edmund, you did! You said that I was sitting opposite you, behind my desk. You said that I was wearing a sweater and that I had large breasts. You don't remember?" she said.

Oh, that. I don't count that. I was hallucinating, kind of. I thought I told you that.

"You did," she said. "Does that mean you didn't say it? Does that mean that you didn't mean it? Does that mean that you don't think I'm twice your age? Or that I'm not over-weight or that I don't have large breasts?"

Jesus, Tammy, you're bombarding me.

"Well, what does it mean? I'm not void of feelings, Edmund. I have an ego, too," she said.

No, you're not overweight. You might be a little older than me, maybe a couple of years or maybe three, I don't know. Not too much older, anyway. And what else. Your breasts. I guess they're the right size. I mean, I can see that you have them but it's not the thing I notice about you so I guess that they aren't too large. They're full. They look nice and full to me. They're the right size. Just the right size. Is that okay? Enough?

"God, Edmund. You make it sound like I'm begging. Is that okay? Is that enough? I don't want you to say something for me because you think I want to hear it. You can be honest with me. Don't say things just to try to make me feel good," she said. "Please."

I'm not, for Chrissake. I'm trying to explain that the stuff that I said when I was hallucinating doesn't count. I mean, Jesus Christ, Tammy. Here I am with my head all stitched up because I saw old man Durkin and I thought it was my father who had finally come to bash my brains in once and for all. Don't you see?

It was only a reality in my mind. Do you get it?

"Yes, I do," she said. "I think I do. I'll know when you are hallucinating because it won't fit with reality. Is that right?"

It won't fit with your reality. Right. You'll know as it happens. But I won't know until later. For me, at the time it's happening it's as real as can be.

"Okay," she said.

I think it's some kind of thing that happens automatically, really. I mean it's no secret to you that I thought my father would have killed me if that would have been him, right?

"Right," she said.

Well, I could have told you that before. That's what I mean that it isn't really a secret.

I mean, if you had asked me before, if I would have seen my father reincarnated and walking down the hall toward me with a cane in his hand, what would I have thought? Well, I probably would have answered something like, Oh shit! He's probably come back to finish the job.

"Well, what about your brother? What about Robert?" she says. "You talked about Robert visiting you here at the nursing home. You said he came to see you twice. But on the records in the office, you're shown as not having any brothers or sisters. What's with that?"

Did I say my brother visited me? I don't remember saying that.

"You did," she said. "You said it."

It's not true. I don't have a brother. He died when he was a baby. I don't remember it happening at all. I only re-member the day he came home from the hospital and little things. I don't think he even got old enough to walk, but I'm not positive.

"So, you were hallucinating about him visiting you here?" she said.

I guess so. I mean Jesus, Tam, yes.

Look. What I'm saying is that if another reality didn't enter into my life from time to time, I think I would go absolutely and completely mad. Insane. Completely insane. Now do you understand?

"Yes, but not the, why, of it all," she said.

Because, Jesus, I've had some strange encounters with my mind over the years. Three breakdowns. Hospitalizations. A family like mine. I mean, I had a father who hated me and a mother who wouldn't help me and who was so helpless that I was always trying to save her.

To be here requires an escape. Think about it, Tammy. I can't even fucking commit suicide if I should decide I want to. You might sit where you are and look at me from your reality and be thinking how you don't want to commit suicide and how that isn't such a bad option to be missing out on. But for me it's a terrible loss.

What do I have? I'm a prisoner of life.

★★★★★★★★★★★★★★★

"What do you mean, Edmund?" she said.

About what, being a prisoner?

"No, about your mother being helpless," she said

Just that. She was helpless. She's not anymore, thank God, but when I was a kid, she sure was.

"Edmund?" she said.

Yeah?

"Never mind,[11] she said.

What?

"Nothing. Tell me about your mother. When did you come to think about her being helpless?" she said.

Well, I didn't realize a lot of things until I've been here, lying around with nothing to do but think.

It would have been nicer if I could have known some things that I know now when I was younger. Like, if I could have watched more of my life as an observer rather than have been so fucking caught up in it. Do you know what I mean?

"I'm not really sure. What do you mean, caught up in it?" she said.

Caught up in it. That's what I mean.

Like, for instance, instead of trying to do something right for my father and have him love me and all that other bullshit that fathers do, it would have been nice to be able to step back and watch him and me like it were a movie. You know, where I wouldn't have been so involved. Where I just could have looked at the movie and seen some fucked-up guy fucking all over his kid. I could have watched the screen.

Of course, maybe I wasn't an easy kid.

"What do you mean," she said.

I used to get these headaches and not be able to go to school sometimes. The headaches used to kill me. They would hurt so much that I would get nauseated. It seems to me that I used to get them from the time I was about six or so until I was sixteen. My whole head would throb. It used to feel like my temples were going to explode and like there was a lead ball in my skull at the back of my head. But then, somehow, I stopped getting them then. Anyway, I probably wasn't a real easy kid.

Maybe if I could have done some things differently then I wouldn't have been as involved as I was. I probably fed my parents what it was that they needed to act the ways that they did towards me. Do you understand?

"Well," she said, "of course I understand what you are saying, I just can't understand what's behind it. For you to expect that you should have been able to act differently so that you could have changed your parent's behavior is a little much, Edmund. Children are not the ones who effect changes in families. Parents effect the changes."

Okay, okay. I don't know what I should have done. I don't know, really. "Maybe you shouldn't have done anything. Maybe you have lived a fine life and maybe you were given little that nurtured. Little that loved. Maybe you came out of your situation better than anyone else would have," she said.

Yeah, maybe. But it doesn't really matter, does it? I mean, so what? I'm not anybody else. I'm me, and this is my situation and I have to deal with it myself. You can't help me. I can only help myself.

"I'm not so sure, Edmund," she said. "I think that maybe I can help you. Not that I can make you walk, because I can't. But I think that I can help you by being someone in your life that you can relate things to. Someone that you can share perceptions with. I think that's important. I feel so wanting, so willing to involve myself with you in this way. You would get the same benefit from sharing with anybody, really. I'm just pleased, though, that you chose me."

What do you mean? I didn't choose anyone. You happen to be the only one who understands my talk. You know that.

"You don't think you chose me?" she said.

No.

Jesus, Tammy, I didn't choose you. You understand me. Other people think I talk gibberish. I told you what Edith did with that tape recorder. I couldn't even understand myself. It's the truth.

"Maybe we chose each other," she said. No. We didn't choose each other.

But, if you want to know the truth, I would choose you if I could choose anyone. I really would. When you roll me over, or help me up, or when you put me back to bed, or when you do anything, it feels good. Your touch.

And that smile. You make me feel like you really are hap-py to be here. Or happy to see me.

Maybe you light up when you greet the other inmates. I don't know.

"The other inmates? C'mon, Edmund," she says.

Okay. Okay. The other patients. You know I'm just kidding.

Maybe you do light up when you see them. I don't know. Why shouldn't you? But even if you do, you still make me feel special.

Does what I'm saying make any sense to you?

"Yes," she said, "it does. You see me as special.

"I just know that I really want to have time with you and see if there isn't something good that happens."

And for you, too, maybe?

"No, not for me," she said.

Not for you? You don't get anything out of this?

"Of course, I get good feelings from talking with you," she said. I feel like I'm doing something that is good for some-body. I get good feelings for that."

Is that really all that there is to what you're doing? Tell me the truth, Tammy.

"Yes, Edmund, that's all there is. That's where I stand with it."

Could I have some more water, please, Tam?

"Sure," she said.

She puts the writing pad down and comes over to the side of the bed. Her hand goes behind the back of my head and she eases me forward a little while she holds the glass with the straw to my lips. When she lets my head back against the pillow she passes her hand along my cheek, slowly. I can smell something. It's fragrant.

We look at each other.

"Do you want me to lower the mattress some or do you want to stay sitting?" she says.

Just like I am, thanks.

Well, what is it?

"What is what?" she says.

What is it that I smelled on your skin? "Just an after–bath oil. Do you like it?" she says.

Yes. I don't remember it from before. I like it. It seems to belong with you.

"Thank you," she said.

I lay still, thinking for a few minutes. Tammy sits. Waiting.

★★★★★★★★★★★★★★★

You ask me all these questions. Would you answer any question that I asked you?

"Yes, I would," she says. "Is there something you want to know?"

No, not really. I just wondered. "Why, Edmund?" she says.

Just because.

"Because why?" she says.

Jesus, Tammy.

I tried to get some covers off.

"I just wanted to know why," she said.

Okay, okay. Because there's something I could tell you. But it's something I never told anyone. It's about my mother.

I moved my legs again, pushing at the covers.

"Your mother?" she said.

I turned my head away.

"You mentioned your mother a little while ago," she said. "You said your mother was helpless."

No, she wasn't helpless. But what did I know about being helpless when I was a kid.

For Christ's sake, I felt pretty helpless myself. Now, of course, I can look back and see that I didn't have to be so helpless.

She was a trip.

"What do you mean?" she said.

A trip. Not now, but she used to be. Tammy looks puzzled.

"I am,[11] she says.

I don't know how to describe it.

I was always trying to cover for her. I was always trying to make her life better. Her being stuck with my father and all. Maybe it was me who was stuck. I don't know.

I used to lie to her so that she wouldn't feel so bad about how things were going. Do you get what I'm saying?

"Continue," she says.

Okay. For example, I guess I was six or seven years old and it was the night of the Halloween party at the park. We didn't have any money to buy a costume. We never did.

The best costume would win a prize. My mother made me some kind of a duck costume. I wanted to be a baseball player but I couldn't tell her that. I didn't want to be some kind of a stupid-ass duck.

Maybe she spent a couple of afternoons putting it together. How could I say no?

By the time I got down to the comer the thing was falling apart on me. The duck feet started coming apart. When I bent over to try to straighten the feet, the whole back of my costume ripped.

It was a wreck. By the time I got to the park I only had one duck foot left and you couldn't really tell what the costume was supposed to be or what it wasn't supposed to be.

Some of the kids teased me about my costume and I cried. What I was crying about was my mother.

In my mind, I could see her looking at these kids' making fun of the costume and she had tears running down her cheeks. She was shrugging her shoulders.

It was the same thing she did when my father harped at her. That look at me and that shrug, letting me always know how sad and futile her life was and couldn't somebody please make it better?

I kept trying. It was like she had no control over anything.

She used to say how we were a family that was filled with love. Sure, there were some things that we didn't have, like a car, but that was okay because we had our wealth in love.

She used to talk like that and I used to want it to be that way.

We rented out our back bedroom to students. That was okay, though. All of the being-poor thing was okay with me.

What wasn't okay was the pain that I always saw in my mother. She was sick a lot, more often than me. And I never wanted to make her more sick than she already was. I was walking on eggs.

And, there was my father. I already knew that I wasn't much good. Jesus, how would it have been if I caused my mother even more pain? When she looked at me and shrugged and those tears ran down her cheeks, wasn't I supposed to take the pain away?

We didn't tell lies, we lived them.

When things got difficult, she used to start humming. When she did that, I used to know that something was going to give. Maybe she would get sick and have to go to bed or maybe she would go into a rage and go around the house crying and screaming.

Sometimes she took the pots and pans in the kitchen and started banging them against each other and throwing them to the floor. It would go on for about ten minutes. Then, as though nothing had happened, she would put them all back in the cupboards and start fixing dinner.

It was crazy, really.

She made five different kinds of potatoes one night when there were only three of us for dinner.

Sometimes, the boarders would eat dinner with us during the week. I liked it because then my father wouldn't be into me and he wouldn't be into my mother. He would lead conversations and nobody would have trouble. It wasn't so bad then. We were all playing the same game, at the same time with the same rules.

Tammy, how about some water, please.

"Sure," she says, "do you want some ice with it? Or would you like some juice?" No, thank you.

"Here you are," she says.

She holds my head forward a little even though I'm sitting up quite a bit with the bed cranked up the way it is. It feels good with her hand on my head.

I needed the water, but it's too late.

"Edmund," she says, "what is it?"

She takes a tissue from the box on the dresser and dabs my cheeks, wiping them, one side at a time. She's very gentle and I begin to cry out loud. I don't even tum my head to hide it.

"I hope not. Your tears are fine. They're wonderful," she says.

Tammy's eyes have a mist over them. She looks happy.

"I am happy," she says. "I've never seen you cry before. You're letting go of something somewhere."

She stands next to me and puts her hand on my forehead and then bends down and kisses me on the bridge of my nose. Her lips are soft and just for that moment they seem to engulf my senses.

"I love you," she says.

It comes through to me softly, in a whisper.

"It was a whisper," she says, quietly.

★★★★★★★★★★★★★★★

Her hand flies as she writes.

"Not much faster than anyone else's, I don't suspect," she says.

Well, it flies to me, anyway.

We stay as we are for some moments. I'm not sure how to read what has just happened. I don't know why I started having trouble.

"Crying, Edmund, is not trouble," she says.

We are quiet again for a minute.

"Maybe it was something about your mother," she said. "You were saying about playing by the same rules, for a change, in your family when the boarder would have dinner with you. You felt more comfortable when everybody in your family was playing the game together."

Yes, it's true. I did. I felt more comfortable when we played by the same rules. It was like playing tennis with lines on the court. When you have the lines, you know when you're out of bounds and you know when the ball is out of bounds. It gives you a sense balance.

"Was that the thing that made you so upset? That brought on the tears?" she said.

I waited a minute, looking around the room. Tammy sat, waiting.

Maybe it was, maybe it wasn't.

We look at each other. She waits for me to speak again.

Okay, it wasn't. It's something else. It's about this thing that she did. There was this thing that happened, but I don't want you to write it down. I'll tell you, even though I've never told anyone else, but I really don't want you to write it.

"What thing,"[11] she said.

This thing. But I don't want you to write it. Okay?

She says, "Edmund, what's the difference if I write it or I remember it? These notes aren't going anywhere. They're staying with me. That was our agreement. Nobody else even knows you can talk."

What do you mean, knows I can talk?

"Edmund,[11] she said, "you can talk. I don't have some magical powers that cause me to understand you. That's why I say you chose me. I am the one that you talk to. I'm thrilled that you chose me. Your words aren't difficult to understand."

Well, how come nobody else can understand me?

"I can't answer that," she said, "You're the one who knows.

"I can only answer for myself. And that's the only thing you can answer for. When you're ready to talk to other people, you will. Maybe tomorrow? Who knows when."

What about tonight? What about what you said tonight?

"What do you mean?" she says.

C'mon Tammy, you know what you said.

"I said a lot of things," she said, "more than I did last night, I think"

I talk, and now, when I ask you something you don't know what I'm talking about.

"What *are* you talking about?" she said.

I'm talking about what you said when I had those tears. What you said when you wiped my face. Remember?

"You mean when I said, I love you?" she said.

She looked right at me when she said that.

Yes, that.

"What about it? Is it all right to tell you that? I do love you, Edmund. Should I keep it a secret?" she said.

She looked at me and then she began to smile.

"You know that I find you attractive. I have found you attractive since I first started to help care for you. Physically attractive, too. You have nice features. They're strong.

"And that damned cleft chin. Broad shoulders, and legs that have a nice shape to them. And, I could get even more specific.

"Oh! Now, is it Edmund who might be blushing?" she said. "Is it Edmund instead of Tammy? Do I see a blush, Edmund?"

Don't, Tammy. I can't move around much and my head feels a little hot. It's from the fall I took. My head feels kind of warm.

"Let me see," she said.

She came to my side and put her hand on my forehead.

"It doesn't feel too hot, Edmund, but how about a cool washcloth? Let me get a washcloth," she said.

She went to the bathroom and came back with the washcloth for my forehead. It felt good.

"Maybe we talked enough tonight. Have you had enough with all of this?" she said.

Well, I wanted to tell you that thing about my mother. But I don't know about writing it down.

"Whatever you want, Edmund." she said. "Remember, though, that it is down on our paper that I said, I love you. It's not really like you're going to be too awfully more vulnerable than me."

Okay, okay. Write it down if you want to. Here's the thing. I had this fixation. You know what I mean? And this fixation led to this other thing. I mean, otherwise, I would have been in school.

"I don't understand," she said.

Jesus, Tammy, I'm trying to tell you. I had this fixation, right?

"Right," she says, "I heard that, and I know what a fixation is."

Okay. I was fifteen.

Anyway, one day I had started for school but on the way decided that I wasn't going to go. Instead, I decided to go back home and tell my mother that I was sick. She wouldn't question me really, if I said I was sick. I could always tell her that I had one of those headaches. I thought that maybe I would stay home and do nothing. I don't even remember there being a good reason that I wanted to ditch.

My father would have gone to work and maybe I thought that also, there was the possibility that my mother would be off somewhere and that I would have the apartment to myself, I don't know.

I was pretty much into, you know. That was the fixation. That's kind of embarrassing to say, but it's true. I think all the adolescents do it, don't you? Maybe that's why I was heading back home.

I didn't do very well in school and I didn't like it much. There wasn't too much in life that I was getting a big kick out of. But I really did get a charge out of me, if you know what I mean. I think I probably did it more than most. It seemed to be the thing I had that felt worthwhile. Do you know what I mean?

"Well, I've masturbated, if that's what you mean," she said.

Yes?

"Yes. Edmund, it's a fairly common thing that people do. Did you think that you were inventing something?" she said.

And then came one of her big, nothing-to-hide smiles.

C'mon, Tammy.

"Edmund, all I'm saying is that it was and is common. I hope it always will be," she says, and then laughs.

Well, maybe to a point, but I think my life was kind of ruled by it. It was my outlet for all kinds of fantasies. I mean, my mind used to go crazy with all the stuff I would make up. I had the teachers at school, and nuns and women I saw on the bus and probably half the girls at the high school.

In my mind, I'd be talking to the girls, they were usually the older ones, the seniors, the ones with the nice tight skirts where I could see their panty lines. I was a freshman. And I made them so they always wore white blouses that were pulled tight and tucked into the waist of their skirts.

Do you like it? I'd say. How about like this, I'd say, and then I'd ram it home and their heads would go back and they would have a wonderfully large smile on their faces and they'd say, Yes, yes, oh my God, Edmund, yes, give it to me, big-boy.

Maybe I was going home to get some of the girls from school. Or maybe I needed to get one of the older women who lived in the apartment building. I used to get them often, too.

What I was probably hoping was that my mother wouldn't be home so that I could get into the top middle drawer of my father's dresser where he kept an envelope with about a dozen photographs. They were photographs of women. Not from magazines. They were real photographs.

This one woman was wearing a sweatshirt and she was turned sideways so that you could see that she had these really large breasts. It just teased you, looking at her with her smile that kind of said, C'mon, Edmund, come to mommy. There was another picture of her with her sweatshirt off but still wearing her bra. She was looking surprised. She was standing in front of some large boulders, pretending like she didn't really know that she was going to have her picture taken. That made it even nicer because she knew she was being naughty. And then there was another picture of her with her bra off. She had one breast cupped in a hand and her other hand was behind her back and she was saying, Now! Come take me now, Edmund. C'mon, big-boy, bang me up against the rocks!

And I would.

Some photos had two women together, one with a hand on the other's breast and the other with a hand on her partner's crotch and they were kissing. I can't even remember their names it was so long ago. That seems strange. We used to do it together, the three of us, in all kinds of positions. They would chant, Big-boy! Big-boy! Big-boy! They really loved me, I think.

I lay there, half erect from memories. "Edmund?" Tammy says.

Her voice sounds distant. "Edmund?" she says, again.

Her voice is louder this time and I look over to her.

"Edmund, honey," she says, "is that the secret you wanted to tell me?"

I don't say anything.

"Please, Edmund. Honey! Answer me. Is that what you wanted to tell me about the day you went home from school? Is that it?"

I look at her but she looks far away, and smaller too. And her voice, it's sounding very distant and like it can hardly make it across the room.

"Edmund!" she says.

I can hear her emphasis, but it isn't loud, really. It's a strange thing, because I can see the strain on her face. She looks so distantly anguished.

"Is that what you wanted to tell me about your mother?" she says.

It looks like she's shouting, but it's coming through so muffled.

"Talk to me, please," her voice says. "Tell me what happened when you got back home that day."

I can hardly hear her. She's growing fainter.

"Edmund! Tell me! What happened?" she yells. "Did you find your mother there when you went back home? Was she dead?"

Tammy looks small now, like a miniature of some sort. It's almost comical.

There are veins sticking out on her neck while she yells.

"Edmund! Did she knot a plastic bag around her neck? Did she commit suicide? Edmund?"

★★★★★★★★★★★★★★★

I can't hear Tammy anymore. I can see her mouth moving but there is no sound coming from it.

I turn my head and look out through the narrow pane of glass on the west wall.

The moon is high in the night sky and a wisp of cloud is moving across the top of it. But still, there is a good amount of light for the night. It is a nice, clear night and it is a light night and it is mild outside. It is balmy. There is a large field with trees in the distance.

And there I am out in the field. I am crossing the field with Tammy. We are both wearing shorts and it is summer. The grass in the field grows up as high as my knees and I am enjoying feeling the blades as they brush my bare legs while we walk. I think we are headed for the knoll up ahead where we will spread our blanket while we have our picnic.

A picnic at night. I've never been on a picnic at night. This is going to be special.

Tammy and me and the basket. This is really something.

We have some wine and cheese in the basket. There is also bread and some fruit of one sort or another. Maybe there are some grapes in the basket, I'm not sure. Yes, I think that there probably are some grapes.

We are holding hands and Tammy is so happy that she is crying. It is a joyful cry. A cry full of joy.